THE LIGHT IN THE NIGHT

MARIE VOIGT

SIMON & SCHUSTER

London　　　　　　　　　　　　　w Delhi

Betty loved the night-time,
for with the night came
the most **magical** stories.

Like the one about Cosmo,
the bear who was afraid of the dark.

Betty was just thinking how much she wished she could tell Cosmo that there was no need to be afraid,

when . . .

POP!

He appeared.

"Cosmo!" cried Betty. "I'm SO glad you're here!

I've been wanting to make you feel better about the dark."

"You see," said Betty,
"we need the dark . . .

to see the light . . .

and the beautiful shadows . . .

And we need the dark . . .

to see the moon . . .

and, oh! What's that?

I think it wants to
show us something!"
said Betty, and she followed
the dancing light, holding
tight to Cosmo's hand.

The light
was twisting
and turning,

leading them
deeper and deeper
into the wood . . .

. . . until they arrived at a cave.

"Well, I *certainly* can't go in there," said Cosmo.

"Don't worry," said Betty. "I'll be right beside you. Your hand in mine, we can do it together."

The light led them on,
into the cave

and all the way
to an inky lake,

where a boat
was waiting for them.

But the deeper they
went into the cave,
the darker it became.

"Oh bother," whispered Cosmo. "Let's turn around."

But Betty knew she had to be brave.
Taking a deep breath,

she turned off her lantern . . .

. . . and all around them appeared the most
magical universe of twinkling lights.

It felt like the safest place they could possibly be.

When they eventually made their way out of the cave,
Cosmo noticed that Betty looked worried.

"Betty," he asked, "what's wrong?"

"I don't know the way home," said Betty.

"Don't worry," Cosmo replied. "I'm right here beside you.
Your hand in mine, we can do this together."

And together they danced back through the wood,
all the while singing,

"Our hearts shining bright, we'll light up the night."

Back at Betty's house,
they saw that their shadows
were standing proud and tall.

"It looks like we are both
much braver than we thought,"
said Betty.

Over hot chocolate, they talked about how
they had conquered the night.

And they felt a glow inside so strong,
they were sure it could light up the darkest dark.

When the time had
come to say goodbye,

Betty gave Cosmo her lantern and said,
"Here – so you'll always remember the light in your heart."

And with a hug,

he was gone.

The next morning, Betty wondered
if it had all just been a dream.

But when she opened her book . . .

. . . she knew that it hadn't.

COSMO'S
CAVE

To *Live Your Legend* founder,
Scott Dinsmore,
whose light shines on
— MV

SIMON & SCHUSTER
First published in Great Britain in 2019 by Simon & Schuster UK Ltd
1st Floor, 222 Gray's Inn Road, London WC1X 8HB
A CBS Company

A CIP catalogue record for this book is available from
the British Library upon request

ISBN: 978-1-4711-7325-7 (HB)
ISBN: 978-1-4711-7326-4 (PB)
ISBN: 978-1-4711-7327-1 (eBook)

Printed in China
1 3 5 7 9 10 8 6 4 2